LOST IN THE LANDSCAPE

by

Robbie Moffat

PALM TREE PUBLISHING

PALM TREE PUBLISHING
Paisley, Scotland Pa1 1TJ

© Robbie Moffat 1988-2019

Film Rights © 2001 Palm Tree Universal
First published in digital form JULY 2014
First published in paperback JANUARY 2019

Typeset: Verdana 10pt

ISBN-10: 0 907282 25 3
ISBN-13: 978-0907282259

INTRODUCTION

Some stories come easy, some from love, others from pain. This one has both, the malaise of the thinker, the anger of the doer, the ineptitude of the combination.

We all get lost at some time in our lives, whether it is inside our own heads or in a city wilderness that is too big for us comprehend. We go nuts, we try to hide, we try to pretend we are sane while in fact we are totally out of our depth and are drowning.

So it is for our narrator. He cannot cope, he runs away, he immerses himself in foreign ways in order to create time for himself so he can heal, feel again, be rational, get shot of his dirty laundry. Yet, he is incapable of doing it alone, he still needs to find someone else to help him stop the washing machine that is going round in his head.

And so to our story. Does our narrator succeed in getting his washing on the line and ironed? By the end he seems to think so. He finds his Paradise and we leave him before it turns to Hell.

DEDICATION

This book is dedicated to Donna Catherine O'Connor

She was all Irish,
as Irish as I am
when you're raised in America
in cold Illinois.

Chapter 1

The spaniels bark, locked in their kennels, waiting for their master to return. It is the warmest winter I have ever known, and as yet there's been no snow. Great broken trunks of beech and oak lie where they've been felled by last spring's gales. The line of poplars running up the drive to the manor stand no more. They came down like nine-pins, not one saved, not one left. We missed the October thrashing of the hurricane that devastated many other counties, for the eye of the storm passed right over us without a breath. But how it rained! For two weeks we were awash. Yet we had neither deluge nor flood like those north across the Channel in South Wales.

My story is a simple one. I am in love with two women. I must get away! I must run away as I can no longer cope with being bounced back and forth as if I am a ball.

It is to South Wales I gaze when I climb Terhill behind our cottage. It is a hill I mount to freedom, to the mists. For there on the hill crest or along the striking edge, I balance and I ponder the New Year just arrived with this old age of hill, the sky, the sea. It is the same, the same as any place may be from day to day. Today a blue clear sky, tomorrow grey, and dark, and sombre. Like some tiny speck, I stand, I walk, I run, or I shiver in the wet of a passing cloud.

I have only myself to blame.

Any individual who desires to be in love with two others at the same time is crazy. Such love is a tragedy. It is not desire that brings it about. It is ill luck.

This is how it seems. Circumstance took me away from my cottage home with Charlie. We have our differences, but we are close. I am the master of intellect, she is the mistress of emotion. We live in the depths of the West Country and it is idyllic. But there is no work, not for me. I am not a man of great working hands, I am not of a will that finds affinity working with the soil. In these times of great unemployment, I had to leave the cottage and take up employment in another part of this poor country.

It was a six-month contract. Work occupied my weekdays but left me free to commute home at weekends.

How I cherished those weekends! How I enjoyed the return to familiar surroundings - the countryside, my possessions, and Charlie.

Then, whilst working in the distant grey city which had everything that the countryside had not, I met Marie who gave me everything that Charlie could not give me.

I fell in love, but foolishly, I did not fall out of love with Charlie.

I commuted between the country and

the city, and the two women remained separate in identity. Yet I could no longer separate them in my mind. I tried telling Charlie about Marie, but she seemed too busy in her own affairs to care about what happened to me in my weekdays away.

Our relationship stumbled on over the weekends, and as time passed, I returned to Marie on Mondays with increased feeling that my future lay with her. I had nothing to hide from Marie. I could talk to her about Charlie and all the things I could see were going wrong.

Eventually I told Charlie about Marie. At first she didn't seem to mind, in fact she seemed relieved that I had found someone to share my time with while I was away. The commuting continued and we all floated along. I moved out of my lodgings in the city and moved in with Marie and began less and less to return to the cottage in the country.

But my heart was torn in two. My emotions were drifting. A numbness started to come over me. I was drained. I would go to work and return to Marie who would comfort me and spoil me. Then at weekends I would be plagued by an urge to go to the cottage, not so much to see Charlie, but to go home, my home, and be surrounded by everything that was mine.

Marie took my pining as a rejection of her that fired her fear of losing me. When I went back to the cottage, she would be detached and distant when I returned until I had reassured her that I loved her.

I do love her. There is no error of judgment. She is wonderful. She is full of passion, care, and understanding. I love her for what she is, even when she is wind and storm and angry with me for being the way I am. At times I cannot get enough of her fire and tempest - it is these aspects of her nature that make her so different from Charlie who shies from argument and confrontation.

The situation continues and I can't decide. I can't give up one for the other. O the conflict! The pain is crippling. At times I barely have the strength to function.

Nine months ago I was ill. I had an ulcer. I could only sit in a chair and do nothing. Sometimes the pain in my belly was so great, I felt as though I was about to die. Sleepless pain filled nights left me wrack by morning. Sometimes I would stay in bed an hour past noon in order to have enough strength to get through the day.

I was proscribed homeopathic medicine. I would have a day or two with no pain, no stress, no upset emotions, then again as quickly as the pain had been forgotten, it returned with a vengeance. I dared not risk stress or emotional upset. I avoided all hard labour. I shied from disagreement. I abstained from beer, hot foods, eggs, and countless other former palate pleasures. I was an invalid.

This, then, is how I found myself in debt. Inactivity brought me to poverty. I sought employment, and this is why I accepted the job that took me from the cottage.

Still ill when I began work, it was Marie who made me well again. At the cottage, isolated and infrequently visited, I had gone for days without food. I had been a vegetarian on a diminishing diet paid for from diminishing resources. My stomach shrank so much, I ate hardly anything.

Marie returned me to eating meat and three meals a day plus snacks until I grew whole. My strength returned, and with it my health.

There are those who will disagree with those who agree among themselves, but experience has taught me that I cannot remain healthy as a vegetarian on a long-term basis. My metabolism won't allow it. Yet most of my friends are vegetarian as I am attracted to the non-violent easy-going nature that vegetarianism fosters in the individual. It is easy to observe that meat works on the body and fills it with residues that manifest aggression. It is for this reason that I prefer a complete vegetarian diet, but nature has decided that if I abstain from meat, I will die prematurely.

In all, with health and love and all manners of distress, I have been fully occupied.

My contract has ended. I have no wish to remain in the grey seaside city where Marie has her home, so I have returned to the cottage and Charlie who has found herself another boyfriend. He lives in the Low Countries, and whereas my commuting between the country and the city is one hundred and thirty miles, Charlie has to content with the English Channel and many miles beyond.

I have my problems, Charlie has hers. We continue to live together as friends. We hardly see one another. I'll spend days with Marie, and then when I'm home, she'll be off across the Channel.

And so we continue, but I know it can't go on like this forever. Christmas came and now New Year has gone. I've returned to being a vegetarian and once again I begin the downward spiral towards malnutrition.

I have to think of someway out of this situation! Marie and I are going nowhere now that I no longer work in the city. Charlie and I are trapped by one another. I need to run away from all this before it collapses around me and I find myself miserable and unhappy.

What can I do? Where can I find peace and quiet from the storms that are wrecking me. Surely there is nothing left for me here in England? But I must exist someplace, somewhere

Now here, two days later on the hill tops

in the mist, I do not exist, at least for the time being. I am part of the landscape. I sit and quietly smoke some hashish on a stone seat topped by a statue of Diana the Huntress. I look out over the Brendon Hills towards Exmoor, the nipple summit of Dunkery Beacon twenty miles or so to the west. I watch the cloud drift before the sun and on. There are no mackerel skies on a day like this, it is a blue punctuated by puff-balls of cumulus. There are twenty bullocks in the field below me, and already there are newly born lambs in the hedged enclosures. A gunshot goes off, a few rooks rise from the woods of Cothelstone. I haven't spoken to a soul for two days, except on the phone, once to Charlie, once to Marie.

I still feel trapped between my existence of living with a woman I no longer make love to, and making love to a woman whom lives a hundred and thirty miles away. I dream of meeting someone else, and as I sit here beneath Diana, I pray for the woman of my dreams to appear. It is no fanciful thought, for the Diana seat is a busy spot in summer. But the third of January?

No, it was not to be my day. I finished my hash-rolly and though a little longer about what I should do.

'Move to Bristol' a little voice told me.

But something louder said 'Do not move.'

I wanted to listen to that second voice, but it was hard at times living in such an isolated place as Cothelstone.

By now there was a chilly breeze blowing through my grey overcoat that I had ripped on a barb wired fence during my climb to Goddess Diana. I rose, and moved off right and down towards the ruins of Terhill House. It had been set alight two hundred years before. There were a few pieces of standing wall, but mainly the ruins formed a grassy mount that fell sharply away. I traversed the field, greeting a bullock on the way.

When I reached the ruin, to be out of the wind, I turned and leant against one of the walls. I gazed back up the slope towards Diana, and lo, my eyes fixed on three humans descending towards the statue from the top road. Three women.

Oh Mohamed, if only I'd remained by Diana a while longer, for my prayer had not gone unheard after all.

Then last evening I met some friends for a drink and they introduced me to Jackie. Life can be a calm humdrum thing, then suddenly! things move fast.

Now it would seem that many of my problems are solved. Jackie has rescued me and I her.

But what does it involve?

We have decided to quit this country and go to Asia. Jackie is in a dire dead-end relationship and wants to go as soon as it can be arranged. I am amazed and in my disbelief I have suggested we go to Thailand. It is perfect for romance with its palm tree beaches. She has agreed.

This is how life can be sometimes. I am no novice to foreign travel, and it should not surprise you to learn that I have been to many parts of the world. I do not go blindly towards an imagined paradise, I go with the knowledge that paradise exists for those who seek it and grasp hold of it. I doubt that Jackie will seek the same paradise as I, for each individual has different desires and expectations.

I know nothing about this girl Jackie. I know Charlie and Marie and understand that they cannot fit into the paradise I seek. They are in my past and present but cannot be in the future which waits for me abroad.

My spirits soar.

Here in England I have been lost for quite some time. Now I have been rescued by chance. Luck has always been good to me and watched over me, and perhaps now I will discover a new happiness and come to find myself.

I have not a thing to lose.

Chapter 2

Paradise doesn't exist on Earth. I found that out from being in search of paradise too many times. There are many places you have to pass through in the search for paradise, and honestly, many of the towns and cities on the way make you feel as though you are travelling the road to hell.

'Have you noticed this building from the outside? It's really nice.' Jackie was happy. 'We're pretty close to the canal, there's loads of places to eat down that way. Have you had a shower?'

Bangkok has its merits. I've always thought that it looks its best from the river and its worst from a tut-tut, the three wheeled taxis you find all over Asia. The tut-tut might have replaced the rickshaw, and good riddance to transport that makes beasts out of humans, but the tut-tut just adds to the smog that chokes Bangkok. I might argue that rickshaws are ecological and that tut-tut's are progress. I might add that sometimes it's best not to think about it at all.

'Are your feet alright?'

Walking around Bangkok can be hard work when you're a pasty white Caucasian straight off the plane. Changing from shoes to sandals is one of the first transitions.

'Lets get out of this place.'

Jackie was restless. Jackie was always restless. She came across as a laid-back sort of girl who took things in her stride. I was to find out that her laid-backness stemmed not so much from boredom but from lack of ideas. When she fixed her mind on something, nothing and nobody could penetrate her thick skull and make her see beyond her obsession. She wanted sun and beach. I've always been more into wind and sky.

'Did no-one tell you?'

She looked at me in her own sly way that meant she was trying to drop a bomb on me.

'Don't you want to see the awful side of me?'

No, I didn't want to see the awful side. I never want to see the awful side of anyone. I like it when people are nice. It means I can be nice back. What's the point of folks being ugly to one another, I can't stand that. It gives people complexes and ulcers and god-knows what kind of diseases, mental and physical. Shit no, I wasn't interested in seeing the awful side of Jackie.

'I'm not all sweetness and light. When I get into the heat, I just head straight for the beach and there I stay. It drives the person I'm with crazy.'

I began to doubt that Jackie and I would

be together for long. The infatuation I had for her was fading. As the sun rose higher in the Bangkok day, I began to see chinks of light that passed right through her. She was as transparent as glass. Everyone has an image of themselves, but I suddenly had this awful feeling that the image I'd formed of Jackie was a delusion. I had been deluded by my own desire for her. I began to recognise a false love, a longing for something, anything, and it just so happened that at the time when I had been in my greatest need for love, I ran into Jackie. Sure, she was all right, she was pretty, but I really began to see her in the Bangkok landscape as a small-town girl who'd fooled me.

The truth was I had fooled myself. I'd expected too much from her. She was really quite a shy boring sort of person. She had never been out of Europe before ... well, she'd once gone camping in Morocco with her half-wit husband, Jonah. According to Jackie, that had been a disaster.

'Except for the sun.'

I looked at her with an expression that turned into a smug know-it all grin. I pulled a few faces which probably made Jackie think I had some or of itch, but really I was trying to smile. I looked away and watched some ants crawling along the edge of a table and marching towards a coffee stain. Jackie had her feet on the table and my gaze followed up her long legs to her face that was resting on her knees. She was inspecting her feet for mosquito bites.

'I can stay out in the sun forever. I makes me feel so good. At home I spend half my energy trying to stay warm.'

No one can stay out in the sun forever in the tropics, and being in the tropics wouldn't make the cold any easier to bear once we got back. We? Once again I wasn't so sure that we would be a we for very long. Experience had taught me that foreign environments have the effect of bring people out of their submissiveness. They become fiercely independent. Not that I know much about it, I can only guess that this happens to everyone. It's not often that I have any idea of what someone abroad is like in their home environment. But having come to know a bit about Jackie, and her being a Taurean, she was horns out, head down, and charge. That's not such a bad thing if you know what you want and you are blinkered to everything else around you, but sometimes their can be too much attention to the cape and not enough notice of the matador.

It's always difficult managing to see who's pulling the strings. Poor Jackie, here I am telling you about her and she's got no reply. Maybe if she'd been a nicer person to me I might have some nicer things to say about her. Somehow I began to see that I would never find paradise as long as I was with her. The foreignness of Bangkok wasn't helping, especially as she was a small-town girl.

'Can we leave tomorrow? Is that okay? You don't mind, do you? I hate cities.'

Jackie, bless her, is one of those suburb London girls who's been more used to an English garden life than the cosmopolitan free-for-all that some of us have been brought up with. She was a self-confessed outdoors person (I speak of how she was and how she saw herself). She was a self-confessed many things, but I wasn't convinced. People have a habit of saying one thing and doing another, not deliberately, but because they have a habit of deluding themselves. I had deluded myself into thinking I loved Jackie, but watching her picking her toe-nails, the delusion was beginning to wear off and I was starting to see everything much more clearly.

Suddenly we heard a child crying. I looked from the balcony of our hotel room and saw an ashen faced young girl being bundled into a rickshaw by a slightly bigger girl who by accounts was her sister. Their mother walked a few paces behind as the rickshaw (yes, there are still rickshaws after all) wallah peddled slowly forward as the younger girl bawled and cried to be taken into her mother's arms. The mother shouted words of reassurance and slowly dropped further and further behind the departing rickshaw.

'She doesn't want to go to school. She wants to stay home with her mum.'

Later I read in the paper that Thai children sometimes got kidnapped on their way to school. Not six-year olds, but girls of twelve, thirteen, who'd be bundled into a van with four or five other girls, their hands and feet bound, their eyes blindfolded. The lucky ones managed to escape, but the majority ended up as prostitutes in Bangkok, or Malaysia, or someplace else in Asia.

'We can go tomorrow then?'

I was not really bothered about where we went as long as it as South. I don't hate Bangkok, I've never had anything bad happen to me there, and I remember when Khao San Road had only two guest houses. I don't think Bangkok's as ugly a city as Jakarta or Bombay, but it's all a matter of what you've got to compare it with. Jackie had nothing but the quiet English countryside.

What had made me want to go to Thailand with someone like Jackie?? Love? Loneliness? Pissed off with the western world? Running away? Avoiding work? To have a good time? To have some fun? To be happy?

It was a bit of all those things, but particularly the last. Everyone has a different idea of what constitutes fun. Some guys like to go around Thailand screwing all the black girls they can get a hold of. I feel sorry for the girls. So many of them want a fareng husband so they can better themselves and get more out of life. So many of the prostitutes are nice girls who have no other way of making a living. Who wants to work in a restaurant tending tables for forty dollars a month. The call girls want to live, not survive. They live for someone to rescue them from the streets or the bars or the tourist resorts. They have the true Asian concubine mentality. Its sad, and it makes me feel that Thailand is a real world where people are trying to make it in life even though everything is against them. In England, in Germany, in the States, we have it so good. In England people are born moaners ... they make me throw up in disgust at the pettiness of their complaints. Call it the white-man's burden if you want. I've had enough of it, I'm never going back to it. I've shed that load in search of paradise.

And what about those guys who the Thai girls date. Sure, the guys get lonely and they need a bit of company, sex, or whatever. But a different girl each night? That becomes sheer body count. They start thinking, yeah, she's got bow legs, her ass has dropped, her belly's gone from having a kid. They start thinking proportion. They start thinking meat. Maybe it's okay to be white, fat, and ugly, maybe Thai girls put on a brave face when they're with white whale meat. But what about the girls' minds?   There's no getting away from meat. Money buys, money buys lots of meat. Fifty baht or five hundred baht, two dollars or twenty dollars, the girls are selling it cheap.

Where's it getting everyone? What are the girls getting from the guys, and what are they giving? A shot of penicillin is the cure all when they catch something. But it's not the girls' fault. It's the ex-Nam vets, the ex-deep sea divers, its the Germans, its the Ozzies, its the Yanks, its everybody. Aids is on the way, and everyone knows it. It's the last of the good old days, and everybody knows it.

But now the Thai girls are angry. The Thai guys are all after fareng women and the women are coming in their droves from Europe and Australia for the Thai men. Thai men are really unfaithful types, they think nothing of marrying twice or three times and slipping in few girlfriends in between. Caucasian girls like Jackie are just pieces of meat. See, it works both ways. Sure, I'm being hard, but I saw so many English women with only eyes for Thai guys. Nothing wrong with getting into the culture, but to see people as sexual objects just isn't healthy. It breeds racism. People are always curious to find out what it's like to have sex with people of another race, shit, I've had my share. But in the end you discover that people aren't that much different and that there are only so many variations and that when it comes down to it ... if you make love to someone, it's best when you love them.

And me? I try to love. Maybe I'm getting older and I've had it too many times when it wasn't love.

All I know is that I hate work. I like sleep. I love the sun. I'm my happiest under the shade of the palm trees with the sea breeze cooling the tropical day. I like sand between my toes. I love going naked. I love to take life slow and take it while I can. I'm thirty-three years old, and if life won't come to me now, then it never will. Too many friends and nearly all acquaintances let life slip on by. Yeah, maybe it's not so bad having your own home. It must be nice having a bit of land and a few people about that you know will die for you. That sort of thing is really good. But not every day, every week, every year, every decade, until you're put in a box or cremated.

See, the Hindus have got it part right. They break up life into four stages. The Brahman way makes education and schooling the first stage; leaving home and traveling the second; family life and the pursuit of wealth the third; and lastly, the giving up of everything in old age to live simply and peacefully.

At present I'm somewhere in between stage two and three. I go through the agonies of being a discontent and a socialist while striving for contentment and financial security. If only I could be a greedy capitalist, I'd be sold on monetarism.

'You're such a restless person, Jonnie.'

By this time we were on the beach of Hua Hin, two hundred kilometers south of Bangkok. I winced and made a face that registered my non-acceptance of her comment. Then I thought about it. She was right in a way. I suddenly gushed with emotion.

'I've never felt as though I fit in anywhere. Maybe everybody feels like that, but I can't get inside their heads to find out. When I was young I used to see them talking when I wasn't looking. I overheard them. I knew I was different because I had been born illegitimate and brought up without a father. My mother and me moved around the homes of my aunts. That sort of thing always left me outside looking in. I never felt as though I belonged anywhere, or to anyone, except my mother.'

'Maybe if you knew who your father was ... I don't know. If it was me, I'd be able to imagine that my father was a thousand things ... rather than what he is as I know him.'

Jackie's father had been through some hellish experiences in the Second World War that had left their mark. But we were taking about me.

'I used to fantasize that my father was all sorts of things. He was rich. He was upper class. He was famous. I've had a thousand fathers instead of one. It never really bothered me not knowing who he was, or where he was, or anything like that. I didn't want to know ... not until I got to be thirty. Then Charlie kept bugging me, telling me that I would never be happy until I found out from my mother who he was.

There was a lull in the conversation. Maybe it had been the mention of Charlie who was still at home in the cottage in England. I still loved Charlie, but in a way that was brotherly. She was such a sweet person who consciously never hurt a sole. I could never grow to dislike her. Sure, she made me angry sometimes because of the way she undermined my integrity, she questioned my actions, misinterpreted my statements. She could make my insides knot up and the acid in my belly burn, but she was never malicious, never intentionally hurtful.

Jackie was staring out to sea. Maybe she had been thinking about her boyfriend back home or something. Suddenly she turned.

'Psychologists put too much value in the notion that women are always looking for a man to be a substitute for their father.'

I made one of my many faces. I was beginning to suspect that Jackie didn't really like men all that much. I felt as though she had been damaged by men somewhere along the road of things.

'Freud. The guy was obsessed. I don't think he liked women at all. He hasn't got much good to say about them.'

Jackie looked right through me as if I was a window. The expression on her face was so distant, I couldn't work out whether she was watching rain or snow falling.

'I love my father but I don't think I'm looking for anyone like him.'

End of conversation. It was hard work talking to Jackie, especially when all she wanted to do was to lie on the beach and sleep.

As for the beach at Hua Hin, it was awash with Caucasians. Apart from the massage girls, the deck-chair attendants, the pony-keepers and the peanut and fruit sellers, it was Europeans, North Americans and Australians sitting on their bums or prostrate on the sand burning up. I had to get out of there relaxing though it was.

'I like it here.'

Jackie looked at me with her big round eyes. She's a very easy going girl. She'd be happy sun bathing on the moon.

In the end we spent three nights at Hua Hin in a friendly little guesthouse where some other (male) tourists were getting into the local girls.

I haven't got much to say about these

tourists (though I was to meet one of them again on exotic Ko Phangan) except that they'd maybe drink too much Mekong whiskey and came crashing back about three or four in the morning. But by then, they'd be docile. The Thai girls would have tamed the animal in them.

There was one tourist, an American guy who obviously had strange sexual preferences. You could tell by the way he talked, and by the way the Thai girls were frightened of him.

The rest of the tourists were as docile as lambs and probably hardly raised a mumble when they caught a dose of the clap.

As far as Jackie and me were concerned, we had our own thing to work out. We'd been out of England five days and we were growing apart.

Chapter 3

We went down to Prachad Kiri Khan.

'Isn't it beautiful here.'

I said nothing. I used to hear the same thing from Charlie, but for some reason Jackie sounded less over the top and more sincere. She didn't seem to be trying to convince herself that Kiri Khan was an idyllic Thai fishing resort.

It was.

'Bungalow?' she inquired.

A rickshaw driver, lying in the back of his rickshaw passing out from the noonday heat, pointed and waved us along the sea-front towards Mirror Mountain.

We checked in.

It was all so easy. Everywhere we went it was easy. No hassles, nothing. It was starting to bother me. (Maybe I am getting old or something. it's been six years since I last took to the road). I mean, I'd never had it so good ... clean rooms ... good food ... traveling had been none of those things for me before.

'You like it ethnic.'

Jackie could sometimes come out with statements that got close to the truth. No, I don't like being pampered and comfortable, it just isn't me. Maybe it is time I came to realise that life doesn't have to be hard all the time. Perhaps it is time for me to take the easy options. Why should life have to be any different or more difficult just because its Asia. Who says that Asia can't be as civilised and hassle free as back home.

'You're confused.'

God damn right I was! The lack of culture change was getting to me. Had I flown eight thousand miles to watch Hollywood videos and listen to English music? I wanted some Asian culture.

'I quite like it.'

Jackie was beginning to bore me something rotten. What was wrong with going to see a Thai movie and listening to Thai music? Nothing. See, I wanted to find some sort of balance. I didn't want our journey to be all education and no entertainment. I wanted a happy medium. Sitting on the beach all day was okay, I didn't mind that, except that I got restless. But I get restless no matter what I'm doing. At least sitting on the beach was cheap and effortless.

While Jackie lay on the scorching beach turning to a fritter, I made an attempt to get some culture by climbing Mirror Mountain. As far as mountains go it was a pretty pathetic one. It was really a rocky outcrop of limestone that looked no different from a hundred other outcrops that dotted the Gulf of Thailand coast. At the base of the outcrop, the river that drained the plain that ran back towards the Burmese mountains, flowed into the sea. History has it that a fisherman some thousand years or so ago came across a footprint in a rock at the top of the outcrop. This footprint was later identified as one of Buddha's.

There are loads of Buddha's footprints all over Asia (Siddhartha was a travelling man). As I neared the top of Mirror Mountain I could understand why Buddha climbed it (if he ever did). It offers a beautiful panorama, perfect if you want to take time out for some meditation. To the east, the sea and the palm lined coast with its white beaches stretching to the north; the bay curving gracefully towards the south, ending in a small chain of mountains. To the west, beyond a small lagoon, the high Burmese mountains rising out of the lush green vegetation of the coastal strip.

As I dragged my wimp body over the last of the five hundred steps to the temple at the top, I passed under banyan and boa and stopped to admire a cascade of bougainvillea and frangipani. The air was full of scent, but I sensed that there was something missing, something empty and hollow.

When I think of it now, I can put my finger on it. Mirror Mountain lacked spirit. It lacked that quality which brings out spiritual awareness in pilgrims and soul searchers. It had no life force. Sure, it had life, there were monkeys everywhere, but there was a feeling of human neglect, a lack of care, a lack of kindness. Despite the flowers and the trees and the wild life, it was barren.

I probably just picked a bad day. It was Monday morning and there were no holy men about as I reached the gate and passed on towards the shrines inside the temple. I pushed my face between the bars and gazed into the cell that housed the sacred footprint. I was disappointed. There seemed to be nothing special, nothing extraordinary about the altar or the footprint that was layered in gold-leaf offerings. There were the usual flower arrangements and incense burners found in all temples, but the flowers looked wilted, the incense smelt old, the shrine looked dirty and shoddy.

But it was Monday. Sunday is always the busiest day of worship with Buddhists. As with Christians, Monday is the quietest.

I left the shrine and sat in the shade of the highest stupa for an hour or so. It was about ten o'clock and the morning heat had already turned the day sultry. I began to nod off in a half sleep and soon fell into a fitful state of perplexity. I thought about Charlie and Jackie and all sorts of other horrible things. It was silly ... but sometimes when the tropical heat takes a hold of you, there is nothing you can do.

I hate it worst of all when I fall into a sleep-swoon in the late afternoon and find myself awake just prior to dusk. At these moments I realise the pointlessness of life, the absurd human goals we chase. The fact that we come into this world alone and depart it alone, and that, here, in the tropics in a rented room, a thousand miles from anything or anyone, I am awake to find that there is no-one I am familiar with, or who I can call upon, to talk me through my fear of loneliness.

Sometimes the whole thing lasts five seconds, but more often than not, it lasts at least five minutes. A whole world of experience flashes before me in these minutes. But always I am reminded of black moments spent in Southern India when I was twenty. Always the same circle of questions that I can never find any answers for. Why are we here? Who made the world? When is it going to end? When did it start? Where do I fit in?

And always, I merely succeed, with a great deal of anguish and pain, to block the agony out. If I awake and there is someone else in the room or in my presence, then the feeling quickly goes. If I am alone, then the torment lingers with me until I rise and shower, or take a cup of tea, or seek out someone to confide in, or share some moments with. I hate the feeling, and I hate the tropics for presenting me with it so often.

Perhaps this is the reason why I can no longer bear the thought of being in the tropics alone and unloved. It is the major reason why I shall never be an exile who prefers the tropic way of life to the security of my native country, for I hate the tropic-swoon. As for the other oons - monsoons, simoons, typhoons, lagoons - I can happy live with them.

As I descended Mirror Mountain I could see Jackie sunbathing on the beach, her long slender body stretched out, asleep. She was soaking-up so much sun, she was turning black. There was something subconscious in her desire to be so dark. I perceived that she was attracted to dark skinned men. Maybe I am wrong (I speak in the present tense because I am catching up with the past, and soon I will bring you into the present). Maybe, as I have observed before, like most Caucasians she is curiously excited to experience a close relationship with a black. I can't really say. Multi-racial sexual relationships have outside pressure put on them that make them difficult to work. I meet people all the time who've crossed the racial barrier, and more often than not they have separated from their partner due to cultural differences. People throw in all sorts of reasons why it shouldn't work. If two people love one another, that should be enough. If they care, then who's in any position to care more. My own experience across the racial barrier has been casual rather than long standing. Maybe I just haven't met the right girl. Maybe I'm too much of a white honkey. Maybe?

We stayed another night at Kiri Khan as Jackie threw up on the beach after drinking too much Mekong whiskey with a Thai guy who took a fancy to her. He was drunk out of his tree. I was pretty close by. I had my share of Mekong too. I let Jackie and him get on with it. It's a free world, and people should do what they want.

Muk, the Thai guy, was pretty well gone when we first met him on the beach. He'd been drinking all day, but when we started on the bottle, we caught up with him someways. It was the ganja that did Jackie in. Muk, in his pissed-up state, went off on a friend's motorbike and came back with a bag of sensemilla. On top of the Thai whiskey, Jackie just wilted. With the joint in one hand, and Muk in the other giving her kisses and stroking her leg, she flaked out right there on the beach. She started throwing up, first the Mekong, then her vegetable rice dinner followed by her fruit salad lunch and her two fried-eggs and toast breakfast.

I helped her through her retching as best I could by holding her. Poor Muk, a moment before ready to come back to the bungalow with us in the hope of getting Jackie into bed, stood helplessly by watching a whole day of Thai cuisine being washed out to sea. He eventually disappeared, and I spent the next three hours keeping Jackie warm and supporting her as she threw up from time to time.

Next day, Jackie-O wasn't feeling so good.

Hardly surprising.

We left for Ko Samui.

All that was days ago. Now, suddenly finding myself in a hammock on the porch of a small hut on a coco palm beach is brilliant! This is the life. What more could I want. Fruit salad, pineapple shake, and a slow cigarette. Bliss.

See how my tone has changed. You have caught up with me at last to find me in the landscape. All that has gone before was mere preparation for all that is now to come. For I have come to terms with paradise. Until now I have been enclosed by concrete, blue walled rooms. A fan going round is no substitute for the real-thing, a cool sea breeze. Jackie is happy. I am happy. What more could we desire.

Content to laze by the white sand shore, I wrote a letter to Charlie, and it made me feel so good, I was further content to do nothing the rest of the day. Ko Samui is such a beautiful island. The cold I'd caught from the fan in Hua Hin has gone, and the cold sore I've picked up on my lip is healing. I was peeling, but my second skin is tanning. I'm starting to feel healthy, less out of place, more in tune with an everyday life of doing nothing, thinking little, and meeting people.

Time passed.

Jackie and I got on with our own things.

'I don't like being called Jackie. I think I'm going to call myself Lani.'

I thought that was great. Why shouldn't people change their names like they change their environments. Lani seemed much more appropriate for the tropics. I decided I was going to change my name too. Jonnie seemed such a little boy's name.

'How about Karl' Lani suggested.

I wanted to know who this Karl was. People always want to name you after people they like.

'O, someone who used to work in a record shop in Surrey.'

I said there were loads of guys in Denmark and Holland called Karl.

'I think he was a Dane. He was tall and he had really blonde hair.'

I decided I didn't want to be called Karl.

'How about Sh..aun?'

I wondered if that was with or without an h. Its easy enough to work it out when the name's written down, but tons of guys spell it S.e.a.n.

People might mistake me for being Irish. I decided against it.

'What about Marcel?'

Sounded too French.

'How about .....?'

In the end I settled for Cole. It wasn't that common. I'm not sure Lani liked it, but as far as I was concerned, it would do for the time being.

I lay in the hammock gazing out to sea.

I picked up Thomas Mann's Death in Venice. It was short, and I knew it wouldn't tax my brain too much. It portrayed the dilemma of a travelling man viewing the world at a distance. I can't say whether I could become infatuated by a young boy, but maybe I've never come across a beautiful lad who has all the qualities of an Adonis. Perhaps it could be quite pleasant to let my affections drift towards an innocent young teenager. I adore children, but to let myself be sexually aroused to the point of desiring a youth in the way I am normally attracted to mature women, I cannot tell.

There are so many unexplored emotions

running around inside me, perhaps an attraction for pubescent boys is an area for some investigation. Certainly, the idea would shock my friends, but they have their own locked emotions that society does not allow to surface. The flourishing of such non-heterosexual infatuations might be too tragic to pursue.

On Ko Samui, the display of mature adult anatomy leaves little thought for the beauty of innocent children. There is a constant display of Caucasian bone and flesh, an array of well formed muscle and toned tissue. It is a delight, a visual pleasure to admire and appreciate the diversity of stature and line of torso and limb. There are many fine faces and many beautiful human features that turn the head this way and that. The eyes become mobile and quickly alerted to the language of body and the speech of movement. Nowhere are bodies deformed, everyone is beautiful, their beauty marred only by sun burn or mosquito bites that linger and itch and refuse to heal.

My cold sore is a blemish that mars my beauty. I have a little sunburn that pinks across my shoulders. I have taken too much sea and sun too quickly.

So I lie in the hammock and finish Death in Venice. The infatuated old man dies in a deck-chair. I wouldn't mind dying in a hammock.

Chapter 4

Lani has fallen ill.

Her timing is immaculate. She had really pissed me off and I had seriously considered packing my bag and taking off for somewhere - Malaysia, Singapore.

I feel as though she's been playing me along, and I don't like that. It's screwing me up. I like the woman, but I can't cope with her decision to keep me at an arm's length. O great, I'm supposed to be this experienced world traveler who can cope with sleeping the same bed every night with her yet at the same time be able to go off and screw whoever I want. Wonderful. But if that's a tactic for playing safe and avoiding commitment, then it stinks.

Shit, I'm no good looking male or anything like that, but I'm a nice guy. Maybe that's what's wrong, I'm too nice. But how can people be too nice to one another when the world's full of others being shitty to one another so they can stay on top. I mean, the thought of it makes my sunburn crawl. See, Lani's been putting me through all this questioning about myself, and really I should blow it all off and tell her to stuff herself.

She's all mixed up, see. I don't mean cuckoo or anything like that, I mean, she's confused. She doesn't know whether she's coming or going and it all stems from a fear of being trapped.

Hell, no one likes being trapped, but I mean, when you go eight thousand miles with some one, you expect to be hemmed in a little because you come to rely on each other. There's no one else really. Sure, it might seem as though there are loads of people about in a place like Ko Samui who would help you when you're down. That's what's safe about Samui. But really, underneath it all, everyone's got their own problems and not so much time for anyone else's.

I mean, paradise is a wonderful place to be. It's full of gods and goddesses, but when you get ill and the reality of life hits you, you see some of these gods as heroin addicts or alcoholics and the goddesses as vain conceited bitches. That's an extreme view of course, and maybe I'm way out on a limb, but I've seen it before among traveling people.

So what about Lani, the new Jackie. What makes her so frightened when I ask for some attention from her? Shit, I'm human, I need love and warmth and affection and caresses and all sorts of comforting. It's nice. I enjoy receiving. I enjoy giving. But it's no good unless it's spontaneous and fun.

Lani's put up a barrier and I'm losing interest. I'm used to being with warm affectionate women who show their emotions and know what they want. Lani's being really cold. It wasn't like that when we started out and I think she's lying when she tells me she's friendly to everyone the same way. I think she's lying about a lot of things and I really don't like her for it.

I hate liars.

But underneath the lies there is a reason. Lani might have cancer. Her boyfriend Derek has herpes and he didn't tell her until after they'd been making love to one another for a year and a half. That was a bastard thing to do. If I'd had a lover I cherished and cared very much about for over eighteen months and she told me that all the time she had had a sexually transmittable disease, and that she had passed it on to me, I don't think I could forgive her. I'd never trust her again. Having a sexual disease is one thing, but infecting and re-infecting someone else for a year and a half without them knowing, that's pretty bad.

Lani felt she was rotting inside. She was convinced she could never have another sexual partner now that she was infected. She had continued to make love to her diseased boyfriend right up to the time we left England. As they both had it now, they kept giving it to each other. On the surface of it, it seemed that it was sex that kept their relationship going. From the way Lani spoke, they didn't seem to do much else together. She said she wanted out of her relationship with him, but she didn't have the guts to face up to it. She still loved him, but it seemed like a love that wasn't returned.

Experience has instilled in me the notion that love can be women's greatest weakness, but also their finest strength. Men shun love, and when they shun a woman's love, they weaken her. When a woman spurns a man's love, it enrages him.

Maybe I'm enraged with Lani for spurning my love, but it's a love that's never got going. Lani rules love with her head, not her heart. I don't think she's been lucky in love. Her head enjoys the non-attachment of her relationship with Derek, but her heart yearns to be happy and free. There was another guy she was seeing before she left England, and she's made plans to go to Jamaica with him when she gets back.

Somewhere in between the two of them, she's promised to be faithful with her emotions while she's away. But Lani's the sort of person who makes promises to herself rather than to other people. If she's going to remain faithful to Derek, she won't have told him, she'd have just told herself. As far as Derek is concerned, as long as she loves him when she gets back, things will carry on as normal. There's been no declaration from him that he really loves her, that he really needs her, and that he can't stand her being away so long. He's not that type of guy. It's simple enough, he's into himself too much to care a great deal about anyone else. Loads of people like that. Chicken shits.

Over the last year, Lani has picked up a few other sexually transmitted diseases from Derek who swears he's been faithful. I sometimes wonder why people lie so much when it makes them and everyone else around them unhappy. Then to make matters worse, Lani had a cervical smear that showed an abnormal count.

Now the fear has set in. A major reason for getting away from England is to try and sort her body out. That means no more constant re-infection of herpes from Derek, and lots of sleep and rest.

That's all people do in paradise. Unfortunately, I present a conundrum as she hasn't come round to seeing that I'm more than just an inconvenience. I want to see her well. I hate to see anyone sick.

And there she lies in the shack as the rain pours down. Her present illness is only temporary. It's not as serious as the ailment she has come to Asia to cure.

Lani was only ill for a day. She's better now. It was one of those bug things that people kind of pick up from time to time in Asia. She's even got her appetite back that is always a good sign. I don't know how much longer I can continue to be a vegetarian. We're both losing weight in the heat and I cannot get enough nutrition from vegetables and fruit to keep the fat on my bones. But Lani's out lying on the beach again, and I don't think she knows how much the tropical sun dehydrates the body. She doesn't like the shade much and seems to have this fixation for being in direct sunlight all day long. She's got this crazy idea that the sun is going to rid her of cancer, but she won't listen to common sense. The freckles on her body are growing larger. Maybe she can cope with the sun, but too much sun kind of does people in. They start getting dizzy spells, and when their ice-cold drinks hit their stomachs, the body reacts. It's all very nice to be 40c on the outside and -20c on the inside, but it can throw the body into a quick fever until the temperature outside and in evens out.

Everyone to their own. I'm not going to lecture her. The experience of knowing what is best for our own bodies rests with the individual. Me ... I like a bit of sun, a bit of shade, a touch of breeze, a cup of tea or coffee, a fruit salad, an afternoon snooze, then maybe a little more sun before it sets for the night. This sort of routine breaks the day up. Sometimes, like this morning, if I get up just after dawn, it can be a long day of doing nothing. Sure, there are people to talk to - travelers, vacationers, holiday-makers, drug-dealers, massagers, bungalow staff, waiters - a whole cavalcade of individuals.

Sometimes I get down to a bit of

reading. There's the daily Bangkok Post that keeps the farengs informed about seizures of heroin, or Thailand's war with Laos.

Of course, it is easy to forget that Ko Samui is a special place. Yesterday some fishermen landed a twenty-foot, one ton shark, the biggest catch for ten years. The island is fairly safe unless you want to kill yourself on a hired motorbike, but the sea still has its dangers.

The last few days the Gulf has been choppy and the weather squally. At night the wind drops, and I guess that's because there's no moon in the evening, while during the day it is out and kicking up the waves.

But in truth, I know nothing of the weather conditions in the Gulf of Thailand, nor of the sort of storms that come flying up from the South China Sea. It's a typhoon coast. But in February, apart from the occasional rough day, it's pretty nice, pretty clear for most of the time. Sure, the clouds roll in from the east and black out the sun, but hell, sometimes that's nice.

I guess if I really felt like it, I could be off snorkeling or scuba diving out on the reefs, but at present I feel so lazy and content smoking the odd cigarette, downing an occasional banana shake, dozing off in the hammock on the porch. See, when you're in the tropics you don't need much more than a palm-frond awning to protect you from falling coconuts and the downpours. Our bungalow has a palm thatch roof, four hardwood walls, a door, two wood-shutter sliding windows, and a small porch with railing which is just big enough to sling a hammock. Inside is a king-size wooden-plank bed with a nice quilted mattress. Over it hangs a mosquito net. The room is not much bigger than the bed, and at the rear there is a door that leads down into a wash area that has the usual Asian bowl in the floor toilet and two taps. One of the taps is set high up and does as a shower, but I'm just as happy pouring the water over my head from a plastic bucket. It's more leisurely.

The sunburn on the nape of my neck has still not quite healed, so I don't shower too much. I've stayed out of the sea for four days now, and it might be a few more days before I can reasonably allow salt water to get on my shoulders. I feel such a fool at having let myself burn like that. I haven't been so stupid since I was eighteen and living on a beach in Mykanos. But I suppose it's six years since I was last in the tropics and my body has lost some of its natural resistance. Yet I still think I was stupid.

My lip has all but healed now. There is a little redness still, but at last there is no longer any scabbing.

Sounds horrible. But that's the way things are out here. People get obsessed about their bodies. They look at other people's bodies all day long, then look at their own. They pick at their sunburn, they scratch their mosquito bites, they come down with stomach complaints, they graze themselves falling over rocks and off bikes, they develop tropical sores, they muse over their protruding bellies, they worry about being anorexic, they just worry and worry over the slightest physical imperfection.

My imperfections are my lip and my shoulder burn. For the last three or four days my skin has been peeling, but nothing serious. My ailments are small. Who knows, tomorrow might bring some other imperfection to worry about. In the past I have always lost weight in the tropics, this time I intend to try and keep what I've got. I'm a skinny bastard anyway. If I lose weight five kilos, you can usually see all my bones. Already Lani has been sick twice, but hopefully she'll not lose anymore weight. She's a tall girl, and being strictly vegetarian doesn't leave her much scope for acquiring weight. Too much sun doesn't do any good either. Dehydration leads to stomach shrinkage, which leads to loss of appetite.

I eat fish that gives me more leeway in eating that Lani who throws up if she eats any meat at all. Strange how the body becomes unaccustomed to foreign substances that the mind has rejected. Lani's been vegetarian since she was twelve. Eighteen years is a long time, and as I look out from the hammock, I can see her swimming in the jade green waters of the Gulf, her long arms cutting through the swell.

Floating on her back, what is she thinking? Is she in Thailand, or has she drifted off to some place where only she can go.

She drifts out of sight, then reappears to float some more. A cloud passes over the sun and the water changes to emerald. The jade returns and Lani wades bare-breasted from the protection of the sea. Towards the restaurant she wanders. Will she order an ice drink or will she take a tea?

Such decisions are crucial in the tropics.

Chapter 5

If you want to kill yourself, Ko Samui is a good place to do it. No one will stop you. Jeep, motorbike, water scooter, you take your chances. A bit too much Mekong whiskey, a touch too much ganja, a few grains of sand on the road, and bang! You're dead.

Happens all the time here. Ninety farengs a year. That's about two a week, and that's the dead ones. That doesn't include the scarred and limping, the ones you don't get to hear about.

Today I met three guys who'd been in accidents and they were all staying on our part of the beach. Between them, they had some nice scars. One guy was stuck in a hammock all bandaged up. Sure, he couldn't have picked a nicer place to be laid up, but who wants to be laid up in paradise.

A few days ago a guy flipped a jeep. Bang! Dead!

His girlfriend held him in her arms and cried 'He's not dead! He's not dead!' She was totally blown. They took her dead boyfriend out of her arms, but she started howling and throwing her self about, and tearing at her hair. Tragic. One moment riding in a jeep in paradise with the guy she loved. Bang!

Life shouldn't be like that. There's nothing more tragic than the death of the young and the beautiful when they've got everything to live for. In Ko Samui the life is there, the excitement, the danger, the kicks. You can go throw yourself to the sharks and barracuda in the ocean, or you can surrender yourself to the snakes and scorpions in the bush.

But that's not the way it is. No one's got time to get out of the bars and discos except to drive at ninety K's an hour to some other bar or disco.

People are just crazy. But shit, it's their lives. It just kind of pisses me off when I hear that some irresponsible drunk manages to kill someone-else and not himself.

No, I'd prefer to take out a little sailing boat and chance it with the sharks. At least you can see them coming. When you're doing ninety K along a palm-grove road and you hit a ninety-degree bend, you're already in the jaws of the shark. It's usually the bends. Bang! Dead!

I'm just content to sit around on Paradise beach or lie in the hammock, or drink some tea, and just sort of watch the day go by because it's pretty damn good. I can't justify my inactivity much more than that. Each day just comes and I take it for what it is. Maybe it could be better, who knows, some days I take on moods that wipe the smiles off peoples' faces. That's not so good.

Meanwhile, Lani takes the sun. Soaks it up like a sponge. Nowhere near saturation yet.

Me, I get a bit of shade during the day and sit and watch the meat fry and brains go pop. Some of the conversations over the tables in the restaurant give a kick, some of them are fairly mundane. It's the kicks I like the breaking down of the soul. See, nobody really cares what is said or to who, because eventually everyone moves on, gets going somewhere else. They take people's problems with them and let them blow off in the breeze, or dump them in the sea. Everyone feels better. Sure, there's a lot of bullshit, but there's a lot of love. Everyone's looking for love, some get it, a few are not so lucky.

On Ko Samui, and at Paradise on Lamai, there's lots of love, lots of guys and gals letting it out. Doesn't seem to solve any problems, but it means people laugh a lot even when they're down. That's not such a bad thing. It's pretty nice to sit with some women and talk about the heart when everyone else is out on the sand having their brains cooked. At what temperature their minds start steaming, I couldn't tell you. The first indication is usually when they stagger to their feet and rush into the restaurant for a coconut shake or a mixed fruit salad. I do it myself. I'm as weak as all the rest.

My lip is fine now, and at last I can

expose the nape of my neck to the sun. My neck is still a little unsightly, but at least I can't see it. The rest of me doesn't look too bad.

In the evening, everything changes. No one can see anything that is non-appealing to the eyes. Ko Samui is full of dreamers. Lamai is a village of fantasy. The night lights. The bars. The ocean.

Always the ocean. There is no way that you can escape the Gulf of Thailand. Ko Samui is right there in the deep of it. The coconut plantations have yielded to the human want of recreation and the individual's search for paradise. Sounds absurd, but there's some more to it. But how can I tell it?

I don't know. There's only me and Lani here as you know. How can I start to tell of Linden, Maureen, Lauren or Steve from San Francisco, or George ...?

I don't have time. I mean I've got all the time in the world, but why trade my memories for the pain of getting them out. I've had enough of all that agony. People can get on with it. All the best to them, I'm right behind the push for everyone to realise their full potential. His or hers. Sure, things could be worse. I mean, you could be on an elephant trek in the north and the strap holding you on snaps. Happens in Thailand. Or you could go on a raft with a bunch of people you don't know and travel down white waters for four or five days without life-jackets or strapped down provisions.

All the best. Believe in karma, and you won't care about killing yourself.

I like life and it isn't too good to think about certain things. The nice side lets you down easily in a hammock or lets you float like a boat on the ocean. I don't want to know about the other side. Some people reckon it's greener, but who wants to be in constant search for pasture. Maybe it's easier being a nomad than a settler, maybe.

On Ko Samui, the days pass like the winds. Lani gets on with her own things. We speak a couple of words to each other every morning.

'Nice day again.'

I answer something along the lines of 'Yeah'

'Did you hear the rain last night?'

'Heavy, eh?'

That's it. We don't touch or anything, we just kind of pass like camels in the sand. We look at each other. We snort, and push off. By the time Lani's had breakfast, I've kind of woken up, had a shower, and rubbed myself down with coconut oil. By the time I sit by the water's edge to collect my thoughts and start to think about breakfast, Lani's got her whole schedule for the day worked out.

Today it's a trip to the waterfall.

Me, I like the idea that I don't know what's going to happen. It's nice knowing I don't have any arrangements or commitments or ties on Samui. I can sit and watch the waves break and neither have care nor worry about what is going to happen next. It's refreshing and exciting.

Okay, maybe it would bore some folks to bite their fingernails off, but then again, maybe these sort of folks should just stay at home and watch television. Thailand's not for them, they wouldn't be able to handle the sun and the beaches and the palms and the pineapples. I mean, Lamai is only a little town, but it lives by providing an easy life for tourists like me. It's a Puerto Villarta rather than an Acapulco. Bits of it are like Hawaii, bits like Guatemala. It's got touches of Kenya and Brazil.

But when you get down to it, it's pretty unique. Maybe it's the way Cuba once was, who knows, that was along time ago.

No, Ko Samui's a pretty neat place and is like no place I've been before. Landscape, seascape, yeah, not so unusual, but the people and culture, yeah, that's pretty unique.

Too often these days people are looking for the things to hate in life. Somehow gives them a kick to find out that there are worse things to dislike than themselves. As a result they kind of make themselves feel good by making others unhappy. I'm not saying that there's lots of that going on on Samui. It's just ... well, every now and then you run into it. I can't think of anything right now, and I guess I don't particularly want to.

I'm looking for the pleasant side of life, and I don't feel that there is anything wrong with that. Maybe some idealist will come along and try to shock me out of my dream state. Let them try, I might get a few laughs out of it. See, the island's a cheerful place. Lots of death, yeah, as many junkies go angel trekking as those that are lost on the roads. That's a lot of wooden boxes at two hundred dollars a time. That's how much it costs an embassy to get a body shipped up to Bangkok.

Some of the people here live as though there is no tomorrow. Ko Samui's a pretty nice place to die - nearly everyone goes while they're having a good time. It can be sad, but heavy hearts soon give into the tropical breeze and the Southern stars. Happiness returns and paradise regains its enchantment.

Sometimes paradise can be hell when you wake up in the morning and think shit, what am I doing eight thousand miles from home? But as time goes by you begin to think that home is where are you are and not where you'd like to be. These morning thoughts are as reoccurring as the afternoon blues that come after a siesta (which I spoke about before). Again it is the notion of loneliness, the idea that you are on your own in the world. It's depressing. But then again, life in England can be pretty lonely. I guess, over the last eight years I've been lucky in love. From the outside my love life probably looks a mess, but I've had a good time, I've had my happiness.

Suddenly the thought of being loose in the world again, drifting like a coco in the ocean, it sort of makes me panic. At least I'm not hysterically worried about making my mortgage payments. I have nothing. Sure, I wish I could afford to live for tomorrow, but it's pretty nice living for today. Especially when the world is such a beautiful place. There is so much to see. Where do you start?

I've been in America, lived there, that's no big deal. I've never been to Australia though I got as far as Lombok once. Shit, does it really matter where you are as long as you know where you're at. Being in Paradise isn't that different from being in hell. I know where Paradise is, it's pretty nice. I don't search for Hell, I mean, there's plenty of Hells. Grangemouth. Hartlepool. Port Talbot.

Maybe I should get back in my hammock and swing myself to heaven. MY neck is better, it's getting just as coco brown as the rest of me. Pity it is such a wet squally day. No one is on the beach - everyone hiding out in the restaurants or heading for town. So far I haven't made it off the beach. Don't see any reason why I should. I meet enough people to make my days happy. I actually spoke to Lani this morning.

'Another wet day.'

I asked if it was still cloudy.

'Really overcast. What you do yesterday?'

I'd hung around the beach and visited a guy down at Golden Sands bungalows and an English girl in Lamai.

'Girl at Lamai?'

I detected some jealousy that I had the ability to flirt with other girls. What did she expect. She was spreading it around with all sorts of guys. That was up to her. What I did was my business. I asked her how the waterfall was.

'Really nice. There were only Thai people there. Being Chinese New Year, all the Chinese Thai were out enjoying themselves. We walked up Panorama Mountain. From there you could see how much of this island is unspoiled. People only live along the coast. We only had a little time there. It got dark really quickly. We hitch-hiked back.

The 'we' was another English girl she had befriended. The whole island was overrun with single English girls on the hunt for Thai boyfriends.

All the time she was talking to me, she was rubbing her body down with coconut oil. Her breasts were a lovely golden brown, but she had lost some weight and I could see every knot of her ribs. She dressed and went off for breakfast.

I crawled out of bed half an hour later.

I'd more or less stopped peeling so I didn't have to pick as much skin off as I had been doing over the previous week. Staying beautiful is such a fag. Shower and rub down with oil. It's routine as any other ablution. But I like it. It's better than freezing your bum off in an English winter. In Paradise you have time to look at your body.

But where has all the joy gone? The happiness of being in tropical heaven? Well, it's gone with the rain. With the rain comes sadness, and gloom, and all the melancholy of a Scottish mist descends on me. Without the sun, Paradise becomes another wet seaside resort. People huddle indoors while the great white surf pounds the lonely sands.

All day I waited for the sun, but it did not come, it did not show. Vain patches of blue hinted how the day might have been, but the violence of the sea, and the wickedness of the wind destroyed all hope.

Another day and I emerge from a night of dark moods to discover a sky of blue and white mingled with an ominous foreboding of grey and black. But my troubles are light, my mind is half clear and part working. I lie in the sand and grapple with the possibilities as the grains of sand slip through my fingers. There is no substance to life, it trickles and runs to nothing in a very short time. It is no excuse for apathy, but the very nature of Paradise is that it lulls the restless into a state of inertia. Sloth like, the individual takes each day as though there is no tomorrow. Each individual lives in the moment of thought, and each lives to quell desire.

Yet desire will not go. It eats and worms its way into Paradise like some disease. It turns the fruit of joy into an overripe poison that courses every thought. Temptation does not exist in Paradise, for Paradise is a place where there is no desire.

On Ko Samui, desire is everywhere. I try to restrain myself from want, but my resolve weakens. The mountain shall not move.

I was a mountain. Now, I am a molehill.

How can I regain my height and my strength? Without the sun and beach, there is too much torment, too much erosion of my will and vitality. I flounder. I linger. I wander like some vagrant along the margin of the bay.

Still, I am not alone. There are countless other flotsam souls drifting on the sands of Paradise. Inertia breeds discontent. Only movement, the spur to action, relieves the distress of idleness. Is that so difficult to believe?

O, to be in the depths of despair in Paradise. Where are the palm trees and the glowing stars? Where are the enchanting scenes of love and happiness of before? Where are the beautiful people, those who once had no flaws? Where are they? Where is Lani?

Paradise does turn to Hell in time. It might be a slow descent or a rapid plunge, but Paradise will be lost and Hell found. It is the way of things. The workings of Paradise soon become plain. It is no longer a place held together by magic. It is a place where the natives work and the foreigners are bone-idle. The natives have a daily routine but the tourists have none. Alas, any movement towards the routine and everyday is a step towards Hell. Routine is what drives people to Paradise. The routine of mundane existence in the common home-country run of things. The discovery of Hell in Paradise is what makes them return to that life.

On Ko Samui I struggle to keep my grip on Paradise. The beauty of the island is not diminished by my own jaded view. No, it is still Paradise, it is still preferable to movement. The effort of moving on seems to go against the flow of Paradise. Once you have found Paradise, stay there. For once you leave, and leave you must before it turns to Hell, you can never return. Return to Paradise can never be, it can never be regained.

So I must take it as it comes before it fades. Eventually pressure will come to bear and I will leave.

For the now, I will enjoy. I will bask in the baking sun, I will roll in the pounding surf, I will stride the margin of the bay. I will be happy. I will give up my desires. I will live in the moment. I will smile and spread joy.

The gloom is departing and I welcome sunshine into my heart.

Chapter 6

Lying in a hammock.

Gazing at the swell, frets of jade domino with the white fume. It is afternoon and those with patience catch the breaks of ultra-violet. The breeze blows steadily in from Kampuchea. I am bewitched by the silent sirens.

As I swing in my hammock I cannot be more than what I am. I am not a person of endless depth and unknown bottom. I have neither vision nor wisdom. I am neither generous nor giving. Yet somehow, Ko Samui brings out emotions in me I didn't know were harboured in me.

The day may creak by like some palm swaying against the eastern breeze, or it may snap like a frond in the give of a Gulf typhoon. However it comes, it passes. It goes with the sunset on the back of the day, and brings with it the arrival of night.

Night brings another life that cannot be recalled during day. For today is Sunday, and in common with much of the world, it is quiet.

When things become as peaceful as this, it's not so bad to go and sit on a rock and watch the incoming-tide wash around you. The force of the ocean is something you can never escape on an island. On Samui, the main features of the landscape vary only in tone and texture from day to day, they never alter shape, never take on new forms. But the ocean, the endless pounding force of the deep green sea that rages and roars, stills and becalms in an instant and in a breath, the ocean is every moment a different picture. From the high tide line, the sea mellows and weakens to kiss and cuddle the golden shore. But only for today, for tomorrow the ocean may surge and swamp the palm grove.

As afternoon lengthens in shadow towards evening, the scent of ganja carries on the breeze. The sunlight streams between the palms and the beach abodes - the palm thatch shacks with their porches and hammocks. And still the sea draws the eyes towards the horizon, then back again to an ivory skinned woman silhouetted against the swirling emerald of the sea, the surging sea.

From such a seascape I withdraw into the interior of my being and gaze arriba at the thatch above. My eyes drift once again towards the place where the beat of the surf marries into the quiet of the far horizon. The sky sweeps up in indigo and silver and rises with a thunder into the grey void that stretches up, behind, and over the palm grove.

Once again I return to the thatch and the thread line of a spider. A very small, harmless spider. There are scorpions on Ko Samui, small, brown, and not so deadly. There are kites, bats, and butterflies, and birds that glow in the sunlight. The tiny little olive-backed sun birds no bigger than a wren.

But it's the people that really hurt. It's painful when Paradise brings together people who strike up true friendships. Everyone is in need of love and comfort when they are so far away from home. It breaks my heart when such friends depart for the corners of the world. When they leave they search for you to say their goodbyes. Sometimes they search in vain and have to leave short notes that do not convey all the feeling that has gone before. It is sad and it is the most difficult of all emotions to come to terms with.

The sense of loss is great. The landscape that was before now seems somehow empty. I try to obscure the human impact on the landscape by gazing out to sea but I cannot erase the memory of people who have made the landscape more than just trees and rock and sand. I would like to be so hard and steadfast and feel no loss at the parting of friends, but I can no longer be so. Half a life of always moving on, of always finding someone else to fill the days and nights is constant heartbreak. The mind can cope with the things that are new and fresh, but the heart shudders and quivers from the shock of the unfamiliar. Perhaps Paradise stirs the emotions and makes the need for love a more passionate desire.

Paradise is no place to be alone. Such a place may suit the self-seeker or the crazed individual, but not the romantic. Paradise is Hell when loved ones leave.

And the sea breaks quietly into evening.

It was a hot day and the evening heat rises from the sand. There is no breeze. I still see Lani around. She moved out of the shack a day or two ago to share with another girl. She says she needs some female company and that it's doing her good. I feel relieved and freed. It has been hard trying to cope with Lani's silence and her secretive ways. She's not a very communicative woman, but then again perhaps she's only that way with me. Maybe she's naive, I think so, but I'll reserve my judgment as I hardly know the girl. That's become plain enough by now.

'Can I borrow some of the washing powder?'

I see her a couple of times a day and get maybe a line out of her. As a result I've clammed right up in self-protection. It makes me feel better because of the way I feel treated by her. I understand her behaviour and that is why I've learned to cope with her pretty quick. (I hope I don't sound conceited. I'm merely trying to state the facts). I look at her and find no interest. Every day she gets a little darker, a little more distant, a little less sure of herself. I feel like an observer who can't take part, so I do not. I take part in relationships with many other people of all nationalities, but I cannot relate to Lani though I know her from England.

But I am a nomad, and I cannot really say that I know that part of England or its people. No, Lani's not all that hard to relate to, we do talk. I mean, I can talk and let my emotions free. But our conversation dwells on Ko Samui, dwells in Paradise, not on some high plane or through deep bond. We are nowhere. There is no reason why we should not at least meet somewhere in between.

O life is too wonderful to dwell on the miserable. The friends that have gone will be replaced. If not, then I will hunt then down. I will go to Ko Phangan, a small island to the north of Samui where the young go. I will forget that I need people and I will go and discover a real Paradise, not the paradise of Samui. I will go ... not now, but soon.

How my passions run when the calm of Paradise is disturbed by emotional brainstorms. Such troubles stir the bottom of the clear green deep and turn it jade. How I wish I could leave the beauties of Paradise and travel on to some more perfect place. But where? And when? And with whom?

Alone?

Loneliness is my reoccurring fear, a blue walled room of nothingness. Some find the courage to tread un-walked sands, others are too frightened to step off concrete. I fear the hot burning of the sand. I hate the hard jarring of the concrete.

Where can I walk?

I will find a way. I will walk forward into a new landscape of sea, of palms, of blue clear sky. I will go south towards the sun and exotic equatoria. I will lose myself in rubber tree and palm grove.

But fate has steered me towards Ko Phangan, and as I wait in the same fishing village of Bo Phut, the island rises out of the jade sea. Five kilometers, or ten? I cannot tell. Distance in the haze of a tropic afternoon is not a thing I can gauge with accuracy. Surely the island lies no more than ten kilometers beyond the northern shore of Ko Samui.

And why do I go there? Some have little reason to travel to such an island. When all is said and done, it is people or money that motivates most individuals to act. Perhaps there are a few who travel to lose themselves in new landscapes for the sake of change. But I go to Ko Phangan in search of lost friends. Yes, perhaps it will be cheaper and I will spend less than on Samui, but no, I go there to re-encounter friends that have left me behind. I fear that I will not find them and that I will make new friends there. I must live with that.

Meanwhile, Lani is left behind in

Paradise. She seeks nothing but the nothingness of everyday existence in Paradise. She is working on the natives and has found herself a D.J. boyfriend on another beach.

That's cool.

Lani has no desire to travel or to explore, she's a home-bod of sloth comfort. Perhaps at thirty, the change has come too late to spark a passion, the passion that eats me, gnaws at me, and at others like me. I have been spoiled, flawed by choice and opportunity. I am a drifter.

Now, on Ko Phangan, I cannot find my friends. I have searched for them, but in vain. Instead I have made new friends, each a little different, each a different nationality. Ko Phangan is not the paradise I left behind in Lamai. it has a different nature, a different ambience. The landscape is more imposing, the seascape more violent and turbulent. The breeze is a constant wind, and the sun has a merciless face. Yet it is more harmonious, more tranquil and serene despite the anger of the sea. The sands are pure and white and soft. The palm groves shelter mimosa and arcacia. Clover seeds and little flowers bloom. Banana flourishes and papaya ripens.

Still I feel the loss of my friends and the sea cannot erase them from my mind. I want to cry but it is my mind and not my heart that provokes the feeling. Thus I cannot cry, I must let time do its work to ease the pain.

So I return to the sea, the white horses and the setting sun. A butterfly glides past. A dog, barks at a man carrying two plastic bags filled with prawns. Coconuts litter the waterline, palm trunks form the driftwood. A half moon stands overhead in the clear twilight sky. The wind has dropped to a breeze and the hostile nature of the day gives way to the calm of night. The dog now plays with a coconut the size of a rugby ball and somehow manages to carry it in its mouth halfway to the waterline. The hills turn dark, and here and there the red flowers of the flame trees break the evergreen. The water darkens to a bluish black and edges into the moat of a sand castle standing like a Mayan pyramid.

Night comes and the sky bands white and subtle pink as the sun finally goes. The palms stand silhouetted black against the skyline. The sea hisses on the waver of the breeze rustling in the fronds. Night is here and only the warmth of the sand and rocks remains from day.

Yet still I concentrate on the days. The constellations are too awesome to describe. I could tell you of Pegasus and Taurus, of Orion and Sagittarius, and of many more. But to most simple folk they are vague names that conjure no images. Perhaps it is better not to know the names of stars, the big stars. But until you know the big stars, you cannot find the little ones. Each new star named has a hundred unnamed closed by. The task is infinite.

So the day comes and I feel less restless. New friendships are growing and the tension of the move and journey are waning. I cannot say whether I am alone or in good company. At times I desire to be alone. At times I cannot bear the isolation. Haadrin is a good beach to walk and offers fifteen minutes of contemplation from end to end. The beach is tame despite the energy of the sea. It's pleasant.

Alone on the beach the desire for company draws me to the beach cafe where I have new friends. I must go as the pull of company overrides my want to be alone. I must go, and I will, and I do. It is too easy to hide in the landscape, take refuge in the seascape. As yet I have not explored the coral reefs and shallows of sea. Perhaps that will come. I will snorkel out and plunge fifteen or twenty feet in search of squid or barracuda. Beneath the waves lies a different world far removed from women and love and all the desires that unsettle human kind. Beneath the sea there is a permanence that does not exist on land. Like the heavens, the oceans are worlds unknown and unexplored. They are not like the cafes, the restaurants of a palm island where the nationalities of the world congregate, mingle, and travel on to other oases, other paradises. There is no comparison.

Yet I am human and I cannot turn my back on my own kind. I enjoy watching the nations of the world playing volleyball on the purest white sands. I smile and engage with the cosmopolitan game of soccer played by fit healthy men. Up and down the waterline they run. For here in Paradise, the young and athletic thrive and grow in beauty with every day. Life on a coconut island is fit for the Gods, and mere mortals are blessed to be free to revel in the beauty of such bounty.

With a diet of fruit and vegetables, sometimes a little fish, and the taking of clear spring or rain water, the body responds. The sun and sea does the rest. A little exercise, a swim, a body-surf, a walk along a cliff path or a hill track, a nap beneath a palm. All these nurture the feeling that if we could always live like this, then we would live forever.

And so we might if we could keep our minds from decaying. In the end, it is our minds that do for us. It is my mind that ruins my health and saps my vigour. My body is strong, it is brown and firm and supple. My infections are gone, my lip mended, my neck healed. I am whole.

If only my mind were more healthy. I am coming to terms with being once more alone, and now, I am enjoying the freedom that the removal of commitment brings. Yet I am ashamed I have not written to my friends, my lovers, my own mother. It is a failing in me. I let time drift by as if there is no tomorrow, for in Paradise life is lived for today. There is no yesterday, each day brings fresh feelings and emotions unknown before. It is the landscape, the seascape, the glory of the skyscape that composes the trinity of our world. These are the forms. Our minds supply the content. Our imagination runs wild and sees the world as restaurants, banks, hotels, homes, streets, cars, and rubbish heaps. Where is Paradise amongst all that? Obliterated by human want to make the landscape box-shape and concrete. Is Hong Kong any different from New York? Is Bangkok any different from Sao Paulo?

What has happened to the landscape in these metropolises? Lost beneath the high-rise and the expressway. In such places men are lost in a landscape of their own making.

Here on Ko Phangan there is a natural world of driftwood and tropic squall. The travellers make castles that the ocean soon returns to sand. It is like all man made things. They are impermanent. They are constructed and then they are destroyed. There is no lasting evidence of human activity. Maybe there is a five-thousand year old pyramid in Egypt. Maybe there is a three-thousand year old temple in India. Maybe the bible records human history, but who can really believe in Genesis.

No, perhaps it is better that we spent

our time making sand castles than building monuments that we think will last forever. They never do. Likewise we do not last ... our time is brief.

But all these things are known. I merely remind myself of my own short life. If I wake in distant Thailand with a heavy heart, would I not also wake in England with the same feeling? Place has no bearing on existence, and my existence has no bearing on the landscape. I am not lost, but in a short while, there will be no evidence that I was once here in Paradise.

Chapter 7

There's something nice about lying naked on a beach. Maybe it looks a little strange, a little undignified, a little startling. But it's nice. Walking around in a g-string looks great on a woman, but on a guy it looks pretty absurd. It's the bit that dangles down in front, it looks out of place, it makes you want to cut it off. Perhaps it's the vulnerability of the dangle that makes the biggest guy look the funniest sight.

I don't miss Lani at all. I'm relieved she's not about anymore. I made a mistake. We all make them, and I'm no different. I guess I was desperate to find someone to help me get out of my situation with Charlie and Marie. I still love Charlie. I still love Marie. I thought I loved Lani, but it was infatuation. We never got far enough into a relationship to open up those kind of feelings. As it was she helped me make up my mind about going somewhere and I took her along. Guess we're even, though her methods of getting me to take her along were a bit cruel. She strung me out on a fishing line that she cut once we got here.

The world's full of beautiful women. After meeting a horde of them in Paradise, I've slowed down. I'm more wary about getting involved in traveling affairs. Sure, I could go to Ko Pee Pee with a girl from Koln I've befriended, but I'm not sure I like her enough. I like her looks, I like her style, but

I don't know her. There's an Ozzie girl, and Alaskan girl, and an English girl all looking for companions.

Yeah, maybe I do like the German girl. If I give it a few more days I'll know.

Like most males, my expectations are sometimes too great. I want it all. I want someone's love and I want it now. Is that too demanding, too selfish? I have to learn to be more patient ... feel my way ... not head-bang my heart into an emotional crisis. I have to fight my headstrong Arian nature. I have to temper it with a touch of Capricorn. I argue with Scorpio and I fight with Leo. I distrust Taurus and I am frustrated by Pisces. I expect too much too soon too fully. I imagine it is a common problem and I am not alone.

In Paradise there is no one to share these problems with. It is the lack of a past that enables travelers in Paradise to be so open. Some are closed - couples wrapped in love, individuals trapped in themselves. But most inhabitants of Paradise are warm and smiling and willing to tell of themselves and their lives. Some are homesick, some are sick of home. Yet they are the worlds' beautiful people beautifying themselves in the beauty of Paradise. None in such a place live out their fantasies in television commercials. They have taken hold of the real thing. It is the education of first-hand experience, it is not the entertainment of second-hand culture.

How I go on. I tell you nothing of myself and of my past. There is no past in Paradise, but there is a past to face when I come to leave. That is sometime yet. I may move beach, but I will remain in Paradise as long as I am not called upon to set up home or take up a job. In England there is nothing waiting for me. I have no home. I have few possessions. I have no relationship to pick back up on. Perhaps I'll go to San Francisco and work the summer season as a cabbie. I have debts, rising debts that ease slowly larger as I lounge in Paradise.

I block these thoughts out. They surface then disappear in a current of thought that sweeps them under. I have enough to live in Paradise for a few months more, and I shall take them. The cold winter months of a northern winter chill me. I am happy to be victim to the tropic sun and South China winds. I am content to sip fresh crushed pineapple juice. I am happy to eat hot spicy Thai cuisine that makes me whole and healthy. In Paradise I am alive. I rise with the sun if I wish. I sleep beneath the stars if I want. I wear little and I worry little over the choice of clothes I have in my small travel bag. I have all I need with me, and I am happy with what I have brought. I am content. I am happy.

I am not looking for an eventful existence in Paradise, nor are those who share it with me. It is a place of non-event. If there are incidences, then they are minor or inconsequential. Perhaps a pet mongoose will jump up and steal my breakfast omelet off my plate, it happened yesterday and made me laugh. Those things don't happen every day and make you appreciate that lying in a hammock is the safest and most comfortable place to be.

On Phangan I've found myself a hammock that's strung from the horizontal trunk of a palm tree that juts out across the beach towards the sea. At midday the trunk offers the only shade and what better shade is there to have than this while the sun burns. I cannot imagine a more tropic recreation than hammock snoozing beneath the shade of a palm. It's leisurely and soothing. It's paradise.

In a hammock I can reflect that my recent life has been bound to women. I have tried to talk of this before. I have tried to open out and get it off my chest. But such thoughts are wrapped about my heart and I find difficulty in disentangling the actual from the imagined. Last night I let a bungalow-less Australian girl share my single bed with me. That was fine.

I have decided. Tomorrow I will leave Phangan and head south ... towards the western isles. Before me goes Betina, the girl from Koln I have befriended. Like many of the women in this paradise, she has been bungalow-less and has had to shack up with a German man who has been attracted to her. The moving of people from bed to bed is free and easy and I cannot say for certain that all friendships are platonic. But here in Paradise, a bed and not a bed companion seems of paramount importance. If one has to share to have a bed, then there is nothing wrong with that. If there is sexual pressure, then an individual will search for another bed. Bungalow moving is a daily thing and is part and parcel of the search for true companionship. Some only seek sex, and most nights, such people sleep alone.

So, as I lounge in my hammock beneath a coco palm, I one-eyed watch the Tai-chi'ers and yoga freaks bend and contort. For some, such exercise has come too late to straighten backs and loosens joints, but for many others it enhances their being and makes them more beautiful in movement and proportion. It is a joy to watch when it is natural. It is off-putting when it is posed and artificial. It reflects a state of mind that is disturbed and craves attention when the aim of martial arts and yoga is one of contemplation and humility. To succeed and triumph over ego, one should shun beach exhibitions and seek the quietness of the forest. There are few with such humility here on Ko Phangan.

And with the toss of another wave, Betina leaves the island and I pine into my fruit salad. I am resolved to follow on tomorrow and see her in Ko Pee Pee, an island in the west. Once again, Paradise has become an empty place. I will stroll the beach and pace the sand to fill the time until tomorrow. The leaving of paradise is not hard. It is the remaining while others go that proves difficult. At such times I cannot lounge in a hammock. I am too restless.

Now, in my restless state, I have by chance made another friend. We climbed a path together to a quiet lonely beach, and there we had the opportunity to talk without disturbance. Far more difficult than anything else on Phangan, it is difficult to find solitude as an individual as there is a constant attendance of lonely and inquisitive people ready to share their time with you. This is a good thing, but sometimes I want to be alone with a single friend I like, rather than with a group for whom I have no passion.

With this new friend I am contemplating going to Ko Tao, an island in the Gulf. I have suddenly put off my intention to follow Betina to the west coast. But only for a day. If I am content and happy, then all is well. Perhaps this new friend and I will not see eye to eye tomorrow and we will go our separate ways - she to Ko Tao, I to Ko Pee Pee. There is a boat that leaves mid-afternoon and I shall take it if I must. For always I must protect myself from emotional imbalance. Every day romance is in the air and as the days and weeks pass, I become more hopelessly enchanted with each meeting of a new friend.

New friend? What do I mean?

I do not know. I know no other way of being non-committal. Should I say lover? No, I cannot say, for there is no time to think upon such out-comings. In Paradise we live for the moment, not for what is coming. With Lani I could not contain myself to live for the moment, my mind was in a world of future. I did not go with the flow. All that has changed!

The sea has not. The same endless lapping of the waves. It is full moon and the ocean is calm and docile. Along the margin of the bay I occasionally see girls that I mistake for Betina. None have her erect aristocratic way of walking. I had first seen her on the small open boat that brought me to Ko Phangan. It was a wild trip of high waves that soaked us all. Betina had sat grim faced while lashed by the breaking spray. We glanced at one another from time to time, but we were both guarded with our smiles and eyes. We had to sit together when we transferred to the small half-sinking boat that took us into the shallows of Haadrin. I baled while Betina huddled on the bench.

We were first ashore and went our separate ways. I searched for a bungalow to rent, but in vain, they were all full. An hour later I found myself in a beach restaurant at a table opposite Betina. We were both bungalow-less and so we were to remain. She had broken her toe the day before while playing volleyball and had gone to Samui for treatment. She had lost her bungalow and now an easy going Bavarian had offered her room in his bed. (As I've said, in Paradise a bed is more important than a bed companion.) It was growing dark and it was the best offer she got, so she took it. I spent the night in a tent. The following day I got a room in a shack.

Betina and I became good friends. We'd spend most of the day on the beach and in the evening move from restaurant to restaurant. She was a very complex woman who showed indications of ruthlessness towards lesser mortals than herself.

I found her amusing.

Now she is gone, and if I were to catch the afternoon boat, I could follow on to Ko Pee Pee as she expects.

But I have also met Lindy. Perhaps nothing will happen and our friendship will become nothing more than what it is for now. I have decided to wait a day for her to think about going to Ko Tao. And as Betina fades into the blue of the evening landscape, I wait for Lindy to emerge out of the sunrise of another day.

So with nothing to do, I deposit myself in the hammock beneath the horizontal palm and gaze out to sea.

The sea. Forever the sea.

Chapter 8

The island draws me like the flight of the sea eagle over my head. I am back on Ko Samui. No Ko Tao ... no Ko Pee Pee. Back in Paradise, back in Samui.

Night has fallen and the last grey of the day fades into the moonlight. The sea breaks calm on the pearl sands of Chaweng. The lights of Chaweng Noi glitter in the spray borne swiftly in from the Gulf. The cafe lights fairy-flicker. The breeze rings a bell on a clock with a chime. Slow ballad music plays from within.

I am outside on the veranda. I am alone as I have been these last five weeks. Except I am not alone. Why should I pretend to something that is not true. Yet it is the nature of my story that I tell you of myself and not of the people who pass through my life as mere acquaintances. I have met a hundred, nay, five-hundred different individuals in my time in paradise. It is a popular place that is inhabited in perpetuity. It is never deserted, never void of people in the manner that an English seaside resort is for nine months of the year. If there is a slack season, then this is not it. There are people everywhere. You cannot find solitude on the beach as you might imagine. Here, on these narrow beaches, it is another Spain.

Forgive me. I jump ahead. I have failed to take you right inside me. I have a story to tell, the story of a romance. Romance that happened to me ... Jonnie ... Cole, call me what you like.

I am not going to disappear back into the void of existence before I have told my tale. Whoever I am, I am mortal and flawed. I have made mistakes. I have learned. Yet incredibly I have been lucky, charmed, and converted to the unconventional.

I have met Katrina.

If I am too vague, then it is because I do not wish to share this woman with you. I want her for my own as I am selfish. I do not wish to tell you how I met her or how we came to find ourselves companions. Let us say that Fate has played its hand and brought us together for mutual benefit. Why should I spoil such good fortune by telling you all that I know about her. I am in a dream. I do not wish to emerge from my happy state. I have met and fallen in love with Katrina.

The incoming surf whispers on the Chaweng sands. Morning has come again. Too soon the night is gone in sleep that I cannot recall. I dream but I do not remember what I have conjured from my subconscious. I am happy to see another day dawn, and I am joyed at not waking alone. I have found love and I wish to cherish it with kisses and caresses. I pray for rain so that we might spend the whole wet day in bed. We have no view from our bungalow, it is the furthest I have been from the sea since my arrival in Paradise. Yet we can still hear the surf, we can still catch the salty breeze on our faces.

I kiss Katrina as if she were a child and leave her sleeping. I am drawn by the sea, the endless sea, and I sit in the pearl sands and pet the beach dogs who snuggle up to me. I am surrounded by docile animals scarred and hacked by beach life. I have thoughts about Ko Tao and how I would like to go to such an island where China Sea pirates beach and bungalow.

This is no fantasy.

Now it is too late! I am back in vaction-ville Samui. The jade waters white-horse in on the palm grove shore. It is still paradise, but I have a longing to return to the simplicity of Ko Phangan and the sands of Haadrin. I was happy there, while here on the white horse bay of Chaweng I feel restless and uneasy. I have returned to a more sophisticated world of motorbikes and telephones. At Haadrin, water buffalo pulled wooden carts along dusty narrow paths. The night was lit with lamps and candles. Here on Samui I have returned to pick-up taxis and electricity. It is a disappointment, but I must live with that.

And Katrina? How can I speak of someone I barely know? She has a beauty that charms me and stills me to silence. Something in her look, something in her blue-grey eyes makes me want to take her in my arms to make endless love. It is an all-consuming feeling that sweeps over me and reduces me to a child. I am awed and eclipsed by her beauty. I am joyed and seven heavened when she smiles. I am captured. I am released. I am a love-struck fool.

Once again my mind returns to the sea, the cleansing ocean that births the most fertile notions I have about my own self, and the world of exile from all that I know. At such times as this, I am nothing in the macrocosm. I am lost in the landscape. I can accept this though love eats at me the way the search for love gnawed at me before. I can cope with the external world of chemistry. For now I feel that a bed companion is more important than a bed.

How my mind changes with every new circumstance. Am I really the person I think I am, or am I an amorphous entity of chameleon flightiness. After all, I am just another grain of sand washed up on the beach. If I am too humble, then it is because I believe humility to be a prudent thing. Too many battle against the tide. They do not go with the flow, they oppose all easy options and solutions and decide upon the awkward and difficult.

In such confusion, my eyes take my mind back to the sea, the endless sea, a sea I can no longer describe. It is an emerald void to me, my eyes cannot focus, my mind cannot settle in the swell or the wave. I drift like some storm wrenched coconut. I bob, I float, crest and ride the chop and lop. I am rootless and fertile in the hands of fortune. I travel on the breeze and current. I marry with the flow until a new tide carries me to shore where I am wedded to the sand. I root and grow and shoot up into an enormous, graceful palm. I am hung with fruit, and I am weighed with bounty. I am the shade of day, I am the silhouette of night.

Then I return to Katrina who is my sun and moon. In the lunar night she is a goddess. I am bewitched. I am bewildered. She mesmerises me with her sweet soft smile. How incredible fortunate I am to have her kiss me, to have her hold me, caress me, love me. How will it end? How will we cope? Such thoughts bring pain. I must live for the moment, the now. There is no past, there is no future. We must take what we have and love and cherish and care for it. Such concerns bring back the joy and happiness that has briefly deserted me. I feel my joy grow once again. Within me wells a great happiness. A warm glow radiates from my heart to fill my whole being. I begin to smile. I start to smell the fresh morning breeze. I feel life return to my fingers and toes. My voice returns, my mouth relaxes, my pent-up locked emotions begin to seep and leak.

Yet I have been smoking too much ganja. It clouds my brain, dulls my senses. I become withdrawn and sullen. My sunshine hides behind grey-clouds of gloom and sadness. It saps my strength. It leaves me weak and impotent.

With Katrina, I question why I am the chosen one. I have little to offer a lover that is tangible and permanent. I am the wind. I am there, but I am not. I have lost my self-esteem. I cannot see myself as I am. I cannot explain myself to myself. I am lost, but I have no desire to be found. My way of life will not permit it.

How little sense I make. I have become obsessed by my own internal world. I speak little about the wild nature of Ko Samui. I have said very little about Katrina. I no longer think of Lani or Betina or all the Thai people who inhabit the landscape. Maybe this is not such a terrible thing. There are too many distractions in life, and pursuit of temptation can lead to the hunting of the snark. Many things are pointless, so that it is better not to embark than to be shipwrecked. Perhaps it is sometimes better to travel than to arrive, for it is the journey that is the destination and not the destination where the journey halts. On Chaweng I am journeying. I have not yet arrived.

Some day I will arrive. I'll reach a destination that will be my last arrival. I will not depart. I will settle and accept the happiness that arriving brings. Perhaps there will not be a hammock or a beach or a sea to take from myself. Yet the thought of no jade ocean turning on itself and on my mind leaves me sad. No storm clouds rising out of the horizon. No salt-breeze through my hair. No lapping surf. I cannot take paradise with me when I arrive. I must shed my seascape and make my way upon the land. I cannot continue to dream lazily into the tide. There is no future in the roll of the waves. There is no past in the pound and the break.

And still I linger on these islands. Two no-moons I've idled on these shores. Katrina brings me joy. Such joy she whispers in my ear when we are fast. I cannot break the spell. I am bound by the ocean and the palms. I am lost in Paradise, caught by the rhythm of the in-rush swell.

But oh such pain, such longing for Katrina's arms about me. I cannot pass an hour without her smile, her kiss. No cigarette can stay the time between, no book, no gazing at the sky. Only the sea, the emerald sea, part erases her smile from my eyes. And when I see her, such joy fills and raises me to heaven. I am once more lost in Paradise. Her beauty is exquisite in all its forms. I am entranced. I am silenced.

The late afternoon surf brings me back to my wicker chair on the veranda. I have the choice of a hammock, but the steady eastern wind blows ten knots. In truth it is laziness that keeps me from the hammock. But having fought my lazy nature, I have risen and now lounge idly in the hammock. It is on the sands beneath a palm, but it is hung from two pineapple fruit trees. These are not ground pineapple but trees shaped like pandanus with yucca type leaves that are barred. It's idyllic, and I must accept it in paradise.

A man leads a water buffalo along the shore. A part of old Thailand saunters on. The children play in the laziness of a Sunday afternoon. The sand and the breakers are paradise for the young. Such whoops of gaiety and delight! Dogs idle on the tide sands catching the last of the yellow sun. Young pups sniff and scratch. Two Thai boys play soccer in the last of the glow. Bathers stroll past towards their bungalows.

Evening is in the wind now more strongly blowing in from Kampuchea. I rock and dream from my hammock. A little girl coyly plays with the hammock strings, then shyly goes. I feel my skin for mosquito bites. I watch the ants marching across the sand. I think of Katrina.

I move into the sun and gaze out over the surf and Katrina comes. We sit in silence, or we break it with a hug, a kiss. I am distracted in the going light. Save me sea, save me from the beauty of a mortal.

Chapter 9

The rain craters in the sand. Even in Paradise it can sometimes rain and be welcome. The paralysis of mind, clogged by the pyrethrum coil of night, is cleared in two minutes of rain. My choked up thoughts breathe deep and smell the sea. A pale grey sea backed by a low grey sky. The palms fan in the breeze still prevailing from the east. Beautiful people wander the shore, beautiful people laze in the sand.

I am heavy with thought. Fortune has brought me Katrina, and I now know not what Fate has intended. When we are one we are the stars and moon, we are the constellations revolving in the night sky. When we are two, we are the sun and clouds moving across the day sky. We are the ocean and the waves, we are the high palms in the breeze, we are the pearl white sands.

Beyond this I cannot see. I cannot see beyond this bay and on beyond the island to the mainland. Or on again towards distant lives. In Paradise I have grasped the bliss, the joy, the ecstasy of being. I am fulfilled, yet still troubled by the torment of the past, the pain of the future. I drift from the fullness of now to dwell upon the black clouds rushing in from the horizon. Great billows of cumulus pushing up into the blue noon sky. Swathes of fine sea mist rolling ever closer to land. I wait. I ponder.

The storm clouds ease past overhead.

Dark green the sea breaks white. The breeze stiffens, the sea mist hazes the south shore of the bay. The palms stand black. Raindrops fall, then stop. The far horizon brightens to a light blue. The sand flies, disturbed by the rain, emerge and bite. I grow restless.

Now the whole sky turns black, thunder rolls, the downpour follows, and all the heavens and the earth is lost in grey mist. Only a jade band of sea with curling rollers gives colour to the tropic day. Such beauty! Bathers riding on the high waves like mermen. O so wet, so wet, and I think of how Katrina's been wishing for a wet afternoon so that we might have a real excuse to stay in bed. As yet we need none. We respond upon a whisper or a kiss. In the morning and in the night, and in between when we might. I adore her.

I wander in the rain. Great thunder roars, the Gods are angry. I am swept out to sea. The tide pulls out, and in the wash and tow I am carried seaward. My hands claw the horses rushing past. My head jerks downwards in the body of the roll. I thrash for life.

And now I have hurt Katrina. I cannot tell you of the ache that has weakened her so. We have only just met. One week today the full moon rose, and in its waxing we have been entranced. Still we linger here, trapped beneath the palms. I have wounded Katrina.

'Then you are married!'

Such a wail pierced the half-moon night. Things went bump, and pop and faster than the night was long. We made wild love, then fell in deepest misery to slumber. We awoke to rain and the darkest morning sky I could remember. And I remembered I had said

'I wish to marry you and have children with you.'

And now in a hammock on the beach beneath a jasmine tree reaching flower, I settle in the shade. Katrina wants to know more about me and I want to know more of her. We are lost in Paradise. We must leave this place as now we are bewitched no longer. Our consciousness is changing. The world grows smaller, and ever smaller. The sky hems us in, the sea comes in too rough for a child to swim. Dropping coconuts fall all about us.

I have a wrong to right before the night. How shall I right it? How can I right it? I've been separated from my wife for forty months. I filled my divorce and separation papers eight months later. Two years later I still wait for the annulment of the marriage. I have an adopted step-son who is now nineteen. We had no house, no investments, no capital. My wife and I now live our own lives. We are happy to be separated as we both have different lives to lead. We are friends.

So I am free. I have no wife, for she is only a friend I see once or twice a year. I have no family as my adopted son leads his own life. I have no family home. I am a drifter in Thailand (tropical wet-sticky Siam). I am a nobody. A sickly hobo pining to the sea.

And now I am at one end of the beach and Kate the other. There is such beauty in the Samui landscape. North along the coast I sit and think. Where is my will for action? A German friend passes me some ganja. He instills some resolve that has rooted in me. I must act. I must grasp hold of my inner conflict. To hell with Fate and angels!

I am angry. I feel over punished for a trifle that does not change our time together. What am I saying? I am a villain. I have severed Katrina's trust. I have sown the first doubt and now she will think of me no more and leave me.

I am to blame.

It was wrong of me to want to give all of my love to someone so willingly, so fully, so totally Katrina. I erred to halt and question our attraction. I've never known such constant passion. O give me Libra!

I am the cause of sleepless nights that might have held more dreams. I am the tutor of the day who kept her in our room. But I am the bringer of encouragement and laughs and hammock moonlit nights. I am the link at last that breaks and frees the light.

Forgive me ... I am tainted by life. I came not into this life in common order. You must remember that I am a bastard child, an illegitimate. I was never christened at the altar. I was not pledged to the church 'til I was four years old. My step-father adopted me, and I religiously went to church until I was fifteen. I was a model child of religious intelligence. I was also very physical. I never liked to fight but I had to fight all the time. At least I was passing my examinations and being first or second with my rival Roddy. I was stronger than he was, but he could just out-run me. We were close. We were heads well clear of Josephine and Christine.

But I ramble. The breeze makes me shiver. The day still wears damp. I take refuge and warm myself with Chinese tea. A fresh wind sweeps through me and I am back in the present. O such joy! I have returned from an underworld of gloom and despair. Rejoice! Feel life in the trees and sky. Blow life! Blow!

I am chilled as the rain pounds down. Welcome to the human race. Once more I am amongst people. Music is playing and I'm released from the simoon. Oh such a simoon bent to torture. I am released by the rain. I am free of Fate. I am back in the hands of Fortune. Love wells up in me like a giant. My strength returns. I will see this storm out and take the morning joy. I will hear the birds and lizards. I will be alive to scent and feeling. I will watch the spider spin and the black ants march on. I will leave the sea and seek my interest on land. Yet I cannot leave Katrina first and I cannot bear being here when Katrina's gone. Shall we leave together?

My time on Samui draws to a close. Never have I found such romance in my travels in the world. I have known brief encounters on the road, I met my wife while passing through a cultured city. But I have never known such deep-rooted bliss in a single woman. I have never felt such deep-rooted passion pass from my lips to another. We throb, we quiver, we cry with consummate pleasure. Oblivious to the world we create a vessel, then fill it with our love.

And now I am the fallen man - Adam cast from Eden. I am naked and ashamed. I walk the beach alone, head heavy with failing. We must patch or severe. She must forgive or we are done.

Or we are done.

Chapter 10

Another day comes. Still we are here becalmed after the storm. I wake to cold sores and thorns in my feet. I am thin and weary. I want for peace and rest. But I crave the sun and so I go forth to burn.

At this prime in my life, I must be careful. I am wary of solar rays. They can heal, but they can also fester. They can set free your hair in the breeze, but they can also frazzle through. I must remember. I must not spend the whole day on the shore.

O idle day. I fester and I frazzle on the sands. The tide rolls in some drifters from the corners of the world. They break and exit noticed or unnoticed given the choice. The nations of the world troop the waterline. The merfolk of continents frolic in the waves.

I cannot kiss Katrina as my lips are cankered. She is my mistress. Such sweet submission! O how wickedly she loves me. O how shamefully I accept. She has tethered me and saddled. I have no regrets. She has bridled me and ridden till I am lean and wet. She has stabled me and stroked me until she mounts again.

So I must take the sun. I must hear the pound of the surf and fortify my energies. The day winds on, and my strength has not yet partially returned. I am worried, but it is sunny.

'I'm gonna go and sit in the sun.'

We are obsessed by the sun.

Katrina sits ten paces off, her back to me, book in hand, facing the late afternoon sun. Her lower body is silhouetted against the white sands. The upper half is silhouetted against the white grey sea. And my thoughts wander. Where are we going? What are we doing? And what do we want?

At last the indecisiveness of the tropic heat leaves us. We desert paradise in search of another. (And thus we take a final journey). Two days we are in limbo before we arrive on the gold bars of Pee Pee. My lip heals but still I cannot kiss her, my Katrina. The sun beats down, the sweat profusely glistens on my limbs and torso. My skin as paled from so much time making love beneath the palms of Ko Samui. I have fond memories of days and nights beneath the fronds; I will cherish my idle days on Chaweng for Katrina has whispered that I will be in her forever, and I am joyed by such a thought. I am still bewitched. I am in love.

Perhaps now that I have found romance, my story is done. I could trifle you with quaint descriptions of yet another paradise. I could sketch the rising limestone cliffs and colour in the endless lagooned lakes and coral atolls. I could take you on a boat to the bluest waters and let you swim with shark and barracuda. I could take you far into the Andaman Sea and leave you there upon a perfect island. I could take you, but I would not dare to bring you back. I wouldn't wish to cast you out from paradise.

Now, on Ko Pee Pee, once more I laze idly in a hammock. I think about my mother. Her sixtieth birthday nears and I am on the other side of the world. If I were a dutiful son I would provide for her now that she reaches pension age. I write a letter and tell her how much I love her still and how I miss her.

Six hammocks sway beneath the spread of a banyan tree. The beo-birds sing and flirt in the mighty canopy. We move towards equal day and night. We are eight days from the equinox, and I am eight degrees from the equator. Every day I expect a hand upon my shoulder and a friend to be there. Lani? Betina? Some other person from my past, my recent past - my paradise days?

I am content that this is not so. My days with Katrina are happy. How could they be otherwise in a place where mermaids need rescuing from the shallows.

We are enchanted. We are fast.

Yet how things manifest themselves with the passing of days. Only now have I discovered the world beneath the sea. Blue florescent fish and bright green coral. Red urchins that look like stones, and black spiky urchins that lurk beneath rock columns. I don't know how to describe such colour, such a world. Perhaps it is no different from the waters of Hikkadua or the blue reefs of Key Caulker.

I cannot tell.

I cannot remember.

Yet I know I must pass each day in some fashion, and as these days pass, I have less energy for the landscape and greater interest for the mysteries of the sea. I am no great explorer - time is against me now that I am older.

'Do you want to go around the island by boat?'

Yes, I would like to go around the island in a boat, drop off the side and dive into the green of an Andaman grotto. But for now I am content to swing in a hammock beneath the beach banyan. The sun is high and lovers swim in the coral-sea like merfolk. It is as paradise should be. People are not lonely here. They are warm and friendly. There is caress and feeling in the touch of a fisherman or a restaurant girl. There are smiles and laughs and shouts of joy. There is music. There is poetry in the voices of the bright-eyed children and inquisitiveness in the alert, obliging, fair and honest adults of the island.

The sands of Pee Pee. How will I forget them?

Katrina and I bungalow on the long beach. The little island of Pee Pee Lay rises out of the afternoon sea. Thousand foot cliffs sweep vertically to the heavens. No one lives there. It is the island where the nest collectors have marked out their territory. Bamboo ladders scale the limestone faces of this tropic island. The swifts come and make their nests with their own saliva. It is a strange fate that man should cherish bird saliva as a delicacy that he makes into a soup, but that's how things are with man.

Katrina snorkels. I laze on in the fishnet hammock neath the banyan. I have had no thought for food or drink. I have been at peace. Yet now that the afternoon has lengthened and Katrina has joined me in the hammock, I feel hungry.

It is a kind of hunger that keeps the tongue dry and the lips puckered. It gnaws at me. It devours me until there is nothing left of me. Then my hunger dissolves into the memory of day and I am satisfied.

This then is my Paradise. I linger and lax on the gold bars of Pee Pee. I am lazed by lightning breaking out to sea. Rain rolls in with the thunder. Droplets fall as Katrina and I huddle in the hammock neath the banyan. We are struck by static as the flying hounds leave the banyan for the air. Bats, the size of dogs, bend the tree limbs. The hammock sways. The lightning lingers on the water. The sky echoes the discharge. The clear rain pits the gold bars. We are damp. We are wet. We are angels.

Such angels as we are not uncommon. We live with the sea-gypsies, the peoples of the Andaman who provide shelter for the nomads of many nations. We are all gypsies here on Ko Pee Pee. We are on vacation. There is not a man or woman who will ever willingly end their days in such a paradise. The call of the sea and distant continents is too plainly heeded. We are bound by Fate and we cannot change our destiny. We cannot settle permanently in Paradise. Such joy and fortune is reserved for purer angels.

I have been a rogue, a gypsy. Now, I have been favoured by Katrina, and I am transformed into a common angel. Katrina is a most gentle angel. She is so fine and delicate that I must lighten my touch and learn to hold her with more care than I would a butterfly. She is as light as Alto Plano air and makes me soar with her towards heaven.

My feet leave the earth. I am borne aloft. I am in her arms. I am no longer adrift in the landscape. I no longer gaze out to sea. I am floating free towards a perfect place.

I am found. Here there are no dogs locked in kennels waiting for their master to return.

ROBBIE MOFFAT

The author was born and schooled in Glasgow. He took a degree in English language and Literature at Newcastle University. He began writing when he was seventeen and has a had a career as a poet, novelist, playwright and screenwriter. He is best known for his feature film work in which he is also a director and producer.

His prose writing as been overshadowed by this. He wrote his first novel when he was twenty two and continued to write novels for the next twenty years. None of them were published.

The rediscovery of his prose work has lead to a recent spate of publications that has lead to a resurgence of interest in his prose work.